Amanda Adams Loves Herbie Hickle

Patti Farmer

Daniel Sylvestre

Scholastic Canada Ltd.

*For my son Brian, whose kindergarten love life inspired this
story, and who will be absolutely thrilled that I'm sharing
this bit of news outside the family . . .*
P. F.

To Antoine.
D. S.

Scholastic Canada Ltd.
123 Newkirk Road, Richmond Hill, Ontario, Canada L4C 3G5

Scholastic Inc.
555 Broadway, New York, NY 10012, USA

Scholastic Australia Pty Limited
PO Box 579, Gosford, NSW 2250, Australia

Scholastic New Zealand Limited
Private Bag 94407, Greenmount, Auckland, New Zealand

Scholastic Ltd.
Villiers House, Clarendon Avenue, Leamington Spa,
Warwickshire CV32 5PR, UK

Canadian Cataloguing in Publication Data

Farmer, Patti
Amanda Adams loves Herbie Hickle

ISBN 0-590-12444-7

I. Sylvestre, Daniel. II. Title.

PS8561.A727A72 1998   jC813'.54   C97-931850-5
PZ7.F37Am 1998

4 3 2 1   Printed and bound in Canada   8 9/901/0

Amanda Adams loved Herbie Hickle.

And everyone in
the whole world knew it.
Except Herbie Hickle.

"Maybe I should just tell him," said
Amanda softly.

"No, no, no," said her friend Penelope.
"You know boys. If you tell him, his eyes
might cross and stay that way forever."

"Oh, I wouldn't want that," said Amanda.
"Then leave some candy on his desk,"
said Penelope. "He'll *love* that."

The next morning, Herbie found
some peanut brittle on his desk.
Herbie took a big bite.
Herbie heard a big crack.
Herbie dropped a big tooth.

"Oh, my," said Amanda. "Maybe
I should just tell him."

"No, no, no," said her friend Ginger.
"You know boys. If you tell him, he might
pull out all his hair and be bald forever."

8

"Oh, I wouldn't want that," said Amanda. "Then leave your math homework on his desk," said Ginger. "He'll *love* that."

The next morning, Herbie found the math homework on his desk.
Herbie copied all the answers.
Herbie failed.
Herbie didn't know that Amanda was lousy at math.

"Oh, my," said Amanda. "Maybe
I should just tell him."

"No, no, no," said her friend Millie.
"You know boys. If you tell him, he might
gag and swallow his tongue and talk real
funny forever."

"Oh, I wouldn't want that," said Amanda.
"Then leave some flowers on his desk,"
said Millie. "He'll *love* that."

The next morning, Herbie
found some daisies on his desk.
Herbie sniffed.
Herbie sneezed.
Herbie blew up like a balloon.
Herbie was allergic to daisies.

"Oh, my," said Amanda. "Maybe
I should just tell him."

"No, no, no," said her friend Christina.
"You know boys. If you tell him, he
might throw up all over the place and
be sick forever."

"Oh, I wouldn't want that," said Amanda. "Then leave a mysterious note on his desk," said Christina. "He'll *love* that."

The next morning, Herbie found a big
red heart that said "A.A. Loves H.H." on
his desk.

The teacher walked toward Herbie.
Herbie stuffed the big note into
his mouth.

The teacher stared at Herbie.
Herbie swallowed hard.

The teacher turned back.
Herbie turned blue.

Amanda thumped Herbie on the back.
Herbie said, "BUR-R-R-R-R-R-RUP."
The teacher said, "Herbie Hickle! Go to
the office!"
Amanda said, "But it's my fault!"

The teacher said, "Fine. Both of you go to the office!"

Down the hall, Herbie said, "Why did you say it was your fault?"

And Amanda told him everything.

"You did all that for me?" said Herbie.

"You almost killed me."

24

"Yes," said Amanda. "Now I know I
should have just told you how I feel."
Herbie said nothing.

25

Amanda and Herbie walked into
the principal's office.

The only one to get in trouble was
Amanda. She had to stay after
school for a whole week.

But every day when she got out, Herbie was there to walk her home.